DISNEY
LILO&STITCH

For information address Disney Press, 1200 Grand Central Avenue, Glendale, California 91201.

ISBN 978-1-368-04034-1
Printed in China
First Slipcase Edition, August 2018
10 9 8 7 6 5 4 3 2 1

For more Disney Press fun, visit www.disneybooks.com

DISNEP
Lilo & Stitch

DISNEP PRESS
Los Angeles • New York

Far out in space, the Galactic Federation was holding
a trial. A scientist named Jumba was accused of creating a
dangerous experiment—a creature he called Experiment 626.

"He is bulletproof, fireproof, and can think faster than a
supercomputer," Jumba said. "His only instinct: to destroy
everything he touches!"

The Grand Councilwoman told Captain Gantu to take the
creature to a distant planet.

Experiment 626 was placed in a tiny locked compartment on Captain Gantu's ship. Somehow he managed to break loose and escape in a police cruiser. When Galactic Control tracked his flight, they found he was headed directly for planet Earth!

The Grand Councilwoman sent Jumba and Agent Pleakley to Earth to recapture Experiment 626.

Meanwhile, on the Hawaiian island of Kauai, a little girl named Lilo sulked in her bedroom. She was a little different from the rest of her classmates and didn't really have any friends.

When Nani, Lilo's older sister, got home from work, she found Lilo inside the house listening to records with the door nailed shut.

Just then, Nani spied her social worker, Cobra Bubbles. Nani and Lilo's parents had died, and now Nani was in charge of Lilo. It was Mr. Bubbles's task to make sure Nani was doing a good job taking care of her sister.

Mr. Bubbles arrived and found Nani trying to pry the front door open. She had to climb through a window to let him into the house. He did not look happy.

"Do you often leave your sister home alone?" he asked in a serious voice. Mr. Bubbles moved into the kitchen. The sink was overflowing with dirty dishes and the stove was on. A pot of stew was boiling over onto the burners.

Mr. Bubbles asked Lilo a lot of questions. Nani tried to signal to Lilo to help her with her answers, but Lilo got confused. Her answers made things seem a lot worse than they were.

"Call me next time you're left here alone," Mr. Bubbles said to Lilo. Then he turned to Nani. "In case you are wondering, this did *not* go well," he said sternly. "You have three days to change my mind."

After Mr. Bubbles left, Nani was worried and upset. "Do you want to be taken away?" she asked Lilo angrily.

Lilo stomped upstairs to her room and slammed her door shut.

Later, Nani tried to cheer up Lilo. They were sisters and they only had each other.

"People treat me different," Lilo told Nani.

"They just don't know what to say," Nani replied. Nani promised that she would stop yelling at Lilo if Lilo would stop fighting with her classmates, and the two began to giggle together.

The lights flickered. Lilo looked out the window. "A shooting star!" she cried.

Lilo pushed Nani out of the room so she could make a secret wish. "I need somebody to be my friend, someone who won't run away. Maybe send me an angel? The nicest angel you have," Lilo wished.

Nani was listening in the hall. She felt sad Lilo was lonely.

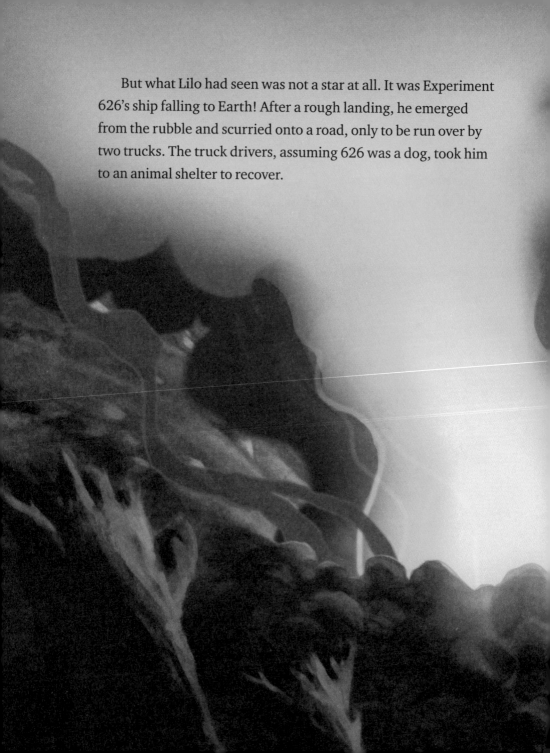

But what Lilo had seen was not a star at all. It was Experiment 626's ship falling to Earth! After a rough landing, he emerged from the rubble and scurried onto a road, only to be run over by two trucks. The truck drivers, assuming 626 was a dog, took him to an animal shelter to recover.

The next day, Nani and Lilo visited the animal shelter. While they looked around, Experiment 626 was trying to escape. Then he noticed that agents from the federation had tracked him down and were waiting to capture him.

Frightened, Experiment 626 ran back inside. Just then, he saw a sign that read ADOPT TODAY. He began to hatch a plan.

When Lilo went to look at the dogs available for adoption, the only one she saw was Experiment 626. The rest were hiding, because they were afraid of the alien creature! Experiment 626 rushed over to hug Lilo.

Nani wanted her to choose another dog, but Lilo insisted that he was perfect. She named him Stitch.

Lilo loved Stitch, but it seemed like everywhere they went, he got into trouble. That night, Nani had to work at the restaurant. Lilo and Stitch went along.

Lilo drew a picture of Stitch. "This is you," she told him. "This is your badness level. It's unusually high for someone your size. We need to fix that."

Jumba and Pleakley were at the restaurant, too. They made their move and tried to capture Stitch, but the alien was too quick for them. When Stitch tried to swallow Pleakley's head, Nani's boss rushed over. When he found out Stitch belonged to Nani, he fired her.

Later, Nani insisted that Stitch go back to the shelter. "We adopted him!" Lilo cried. "Dad said 'ohana means family! Family means nobody gets left behind or forgotten."

Nani knew Lilo was right. She agreed to let Stitch stay.

At bedtime, Lilo found a book called *The Ugly Duckling*,
the story of a little duck who was sad because nobody wanted
him. But then the duckling's family found him, and the ugly
duckling was happy, because he knew where he belonged.
Even though Stitch was destructive, he wished he had
somewhere to belong, too.

The next day, Nani's friend David suggested they go surfing together. The four of them paddled out to enjoy the ocean.

Jumba and Pleakley had tracked Stitch to the beach and saw their chance. Jumba tried to capture Stitch by pulling him under the water. Lilo got pulled under with him! Nani saved Lilo and brought her back to the beach. David had to save Stitch, because Stitch couldn't swim!

Unfortunately, Mr. Bubbles arrived at the beach just in time to see the whole mess. He decided that he would take Lilo away to a new family.

When Nani and Lilo returned home, they were both very sad. Later, Lilo told Stitch that she knew he only wrecked things because he missed his family. Stitch knew it would be best for Lilo if he left. He disappeared into the night with *The Ugly Duckling* tucked under his arm.

Stitch opened the book to the page on which the ugly duckling could not find his family. "Lost," he whispered sadly.

The next morning, Lilo told Nani Stitch was gone. Just then, there was a knock at the door. It was David. He had found a job for Nani. The two told Lilo to stay in the house and rushed off. This was their last chance to keep Nani and Lilo together!

Meanwhile, in the forest, Stitch was in trouble. Jumba had found him and was doing his best to capture the creature. Stitch headed for Lilo's house. Jumba was right behind him!

Stitch ran into Lilo's house. The aliens were right behind him. "Ha!" Jumba cried. "Hiding behind your little friend won't help."

Lilo picked up the phone and called Mr. Bubbles for help. "Aliens are attacking my house! They want my dog!"

Pleakley tried to stop Jumba and Stitch from fighting, but they wouldn't listen. They were destroying the house. Pleakley was able to get Lilo out of the house before Jumba and Stitch blew it to bits.

Happy to have gotten the job, Nani arrived home—just in time to see Mr. Bubbles preparing to take Lilo away forever.

Suddenly, a net fell from the sky, capturing both Lilo and Stitch. Captain Gantu had snared them! Stitch escaped, but the ship took off with Lilo inside!

Nani saw everything. She chased after Lilo, but she was too late.

At that moment, Jumba and Pleakley caught up with
Stitch and captured him. Stitch convinced them to rescue Lilo
by repeating what she had told him: "'*Ohana* means family.
Family means nobody gets left behind . . . or forgotten."

Nani, Stitch, and the aliens piled into Jumba's spaceship
and sped away.

Soon they caught up to Captain Gantu's ship. Stitch jumped out to try to rescue Lilo, but he fell to the ground instead. Spotting a volcano, Stitch had an idea. He jumped into the volcano and was propelled high into the air by the eruption. He landed on Gantu's ship and rescued Lilo. She was safe and sound!

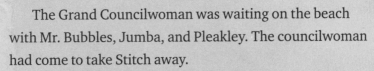

The Grand Councilwoman was waiting on the beach with Mr. Bubbles, Jumba, and Pleakley. The councilwoman had come to take Stitch away.

"This is my family," Stitch said. "I found it on my own."

Lilo showed Stitch's ownership papers from the shelter to prove he belonged with her. The aliens agreed to let Stitch stay on Earth, with Lilo as his caretaker. Cobra Bubbles also realized that Lilo belonged with her family.

They all lived happily ever after.